# Flower Girl

# Praise for Storyshares

"One of the brightest innovators and game-changers in the education industry."
– Forbes

"Your success in applying research-validated practices to promote literacy serves as a valuable model for other organizations seeking to create evidence-based literacy programs."
- Library of Congress

"We need powerful social and educational innovation, and Storyshares is breaking new ground. The organization addresses critical problems facing our students and teachers. I am excited about the strategies it brings to the collective work of making sure every student has an equal chance in life."
– Teach For America

"It's the perfect idea. There's really nothing like this. I mean, wow, this will be a wonderful experience for young people."
- Andrea Davis Pinkney, Executive Director, Scholastic

"Reading for meaning opens opportunities for a lifetime of learning. Providing emerging readers with engaging texts that are designed to offer both challenges and support for each individual will improve their lives for years to come. Storyshares is a wonderful start."
- David Rose, Co-founder of CAST & UDL

# Flower Girl

Frida Pankiewitz

A Storyshares book

Storyshares

Story Share, Inc.

24 N. Bryn Mawr Avenue #340

Bryn Mawr, PA 19010-3304

www.storyshares.org


*Inspiring reading with a new kind of book.*

**Interest Level:** Late Elementary

**Grade Level Equivalent:** 1.9


9798885979542

Book design by Storyshares

Storyshares Presents

# Chapter One

## Lola

FLOWER GIRL ISN'T REAL.

She brings us daisies. She brings us daffodils. She brings us roses. All kinds of beautiful flowers.

But no one has ever seen her. No one knows who she is.

So she does not exist.

She is a fairytale. A bedtime story.

*

When I was five, I saw her.

It was a moonlit night. I couldn't sleep. I looked out the window.

Maybe I was looking for a shooting star. Maybe for something else. I don't know anymore.

What I saw was much better. Better than anything I could have hoped for.

We didn't have a garden. There was a small, gray driveway, but that was all. That night, I saw something colorful down there.

I had never seen any color in our yard. Especially not at night. So I looked closer.

What I saw amazed me. My mouth fell open. My eyes grew wide.

On our doorstep stood a small girl. Even smaller than me. And I was only five, and very small.

But there she stood. She looked older. Not as young as her size would suggest. She looked like a really small adult woman.

I stared, and I stared, and I stared.

That was when she raised her head up. She looked at me. And that look was so intense, I can still remember it today.

I don't know what color her eyes were. It didn't matter. Her eyes stared right into my soul.

She winked. I blinked. Then she was gone.

*

The next day, I found a daisy on my pillow. Next to it, there was a small piece of paper. It said:

*For being curious.*

*Flower Girl*

Over the next month, our garden began to bloom. Before, there was only gray. Now, there were flowers. Specks of green, red, orange, and pink. All the colors your heart can dream up.

The daisies were my favorite. They sang to me when no one else was near.

They sang of freedom. They sang of the rain they drank. The earth they grew in. The routes their seeds had traveled.

No one believed me when I told the story. My parents said it was a dream. My classmates laughed. My older brother thought I had made up the story.

But I know what I saw. I know it in my heart. I feel it in my soul.

What I saw that night was real. It wasn't a dream. It wasn't made up.

Flower Girl is real.

And one day, I will find her.

# Chapter Two

# Charlie

HE WAS NEVER A positive guy.

From day one, life was hard. Every problem in the world had been thrown at him. He often asked himself if he was fate's personal chew toy.

He had called his dog Fate for that very reason. Her favorite toy was a squeaking cactus. It was her fourth one. That was because the first three cactuses had been ripped apart by Fate's sharp teeth.

Favorite chew toy, indeed.

He was too young to remember the accident. It had happened before he was one. All he knew were the stories other people told him.

His parents had died a quick death.

Nothing could be done to save them.

He barely survived.

His spine was shattered.

He could not remember the accident itself. But he could feel the consequences very well. They haunted him every day. He could not live a single second without being reminded of them. Like a ghost hanging over his head.

And so he lived in that life. In that body that he couldn't move. But his heart was never in it. He lived to survive. But there was no feeling in it.

No pain. No anger. No joy. No laughter. Just being alive.

Now, he's twenty-two. He still lives with his grandma. The apartment is too small. The money is too little. But they make do.

They survive.

\*

Up until he was twelve, Charlie hadn't smiled once. There was no reason to. He lived, and that was enough.

But then it was his twelfth birthday.

The whole day, his grandma had been fidgety. She had walked to the window. She had looked out, sighed, and walked back. She cleaned up the apartment. Walked back to the window.

It went like this for a while.

And then the doorbell rang.

The first thing Charlie heard was quiet sniffing. Then there was a little bark. Then a voice said, "Down, girl!"

A small bundle of fur ran around the corner. It jumped into Charlie's lap. It barked. It licked Charlie's face.

It would take a long time for Fate to be trained. She needed to learn everything Charlie could not do by himself.

But in this moment, there was a puppy sitting in his lap. A puppy who licked his face. A puppy who would cuddle into his blanket. A puppy who loved him without any "buts."

Charlie smiled.

*

When Charlie woke up the next morning, there was an orange flower on his pillow. Next to it was a small note.

*To hope. May you never give it up.*

*Flower Girl*

From that day on, whenever he smiled he would find a new flower. They never wilted. They stayed fresh and healthy forever.

And every time he smiled, it got a little easier. His heart became a little lighter.

Now, Charlie has two boxes filled with little notes. His room is as colorful as a rainbow.

*

The girl appears on his doorstep without warning. She rings the doorbell while his grandma is away. So Charlie has to go and open the door himself.

Her mouth is stretched into a wide grin. Her curly brown hair is pulled into a high ponytail. She looks like she can never be anything but happy.

"Hi! So, I heard you got flowers, too! I want to find her. Do you think you can help me?" she asks.

This is how she introduces herself.

After that, they get to talking. She tells him about her life. How she saw Flower Girl when she was five. How no one ever believed her. How she is sure she will find her.

It was something Charlie never thought about. For him, the flowers were a nice reminder. They showed him that there was someone who cared. They told him to laugh more. But he had never, ever thought about the girl behind them.

So he tells the girl about his messages. He shows her the boxes full of notes. The flowers decorating his room.

She is a good listener.

# Chapter Three

# Jae

THEIR LIFE HAS ALWAYS been easy.

They grew up well fed. Cared for. Sheltered. Their parents protected them wherever they went.

But sometimes, it was just too much. If everyone you meet, every place you go, is a danger... then what do you do?

Their parents are always scared. For them. For their future. Their friends.

Whatever Jae does, their parents care.

"Jae, where are you going?"

"I'm not sure that's good for you."

"But be sure to be back early!"

"Careful, that's hot."

They are seventeen now. They can take care of themselves. At least with some things.

Of course, they are grateful to their parents. But there are times when they hate them. When their hate overwhelms them completely.

Their parents are always worried and scared. But that also means they depend on prejudices. Stereotypes.

Jae hates that.

How often have their parents told them not to befriend someone? Because "she is dangerous." Or "he isn't a good influence."

How often were they not allowed to do something?

Dogs are dangerous. They can bite. Don't get too close to that bird. It could hurt you.

But the bird is dying. It is caught in a net. Bound to the rails. Soon, the train will come.

This is the first time they disobey their parents. The first time they do what their parents don't want them to do.

Jae has grown up sheltered. Protected. Loved. But they have also grown up understanding something.

Not everyone has this. Not everyone has a house. Not everyone has food. Not everyone has someone to protect them. To care.

Jae has all of this and more. And they have more than enough of it.

So they swore to themselves: Whenever someone needs it, they will give them shelter. Warmth. Food.

Because if they have so much of it, then why not share?

The bird survives.

*

Jae doesn't find their first note on their bed. Their message is given to them by a small bird. Another, larger bird brings a yellow tulip.

*Sharing is caring. You did good.*

*Flower Girl*

They smile. Their heart warms a little.

The note finds a space on their wall. The tulip gets its own little vase. Both will soon be joined by many more. *

The girl says her name is Lola.

She is beautiful. Her eyes glitter golden in the sun.

Everything about her is warm. Her brown skin. Her dimples. Her voice.

Jae stares at her, fascinated.

Flower Girl. That is who she is looking for.

Jae doesn't really know how Lola heard about their notes. But they tell her all they know.

It isn't really much. They were always happy when they got a new flower. A new message.

It showed them that what they were doing was right. Good. Helping.

But even when they thought about so much, they had never thought about her.

They had helped so many people. So many animals. But they had completely forgotten about her. The girl who made them help in the first place.

# Chapter Four

# Mathilda

MATHILDA IS OLD.

That is what everyone tells her. That is what she knows.

She is old. Old-fashioned. Fragile. She can't care for herself. (That is what they say.)

She must be stuck in the past. Her values must be traditional. There is no place for anything modern in her mind.

A good housewife. Brainwashed. Dependent on her husband.

Her bones must be brittle. Close to breaking. She cannot carry her bag on her own. She does not understand technology. (That is what they think.)

This is the truth:

She never married. She moved out when she was sixteen. She has had a girlfriend ("roommate") for seventy years now.

She goes to the gym every week. She programmed her own computer. It was built from pieces of trash that she found.

Flower Girl has always been a part of her life.

From the very first time she said the word "no," the messages have come to Mathilda.

When she moved in with her girlfriend, she found a red rose. Then she built her computer. A daffodil lay on it the next day. A daisy, dyed blue with ink, was lying on her bed one day. That was after she had cut her hair off completely.

She remembers every note Flower Girl ever sent her. And for every message she got, she sent one back.

*Thank you for making me smile.*

*Your message was the best thing today.*

*The blue daisy was wonderful. Thank you so much.*

After some time, they started writing longer letters. By now, each note they send is a page long. Flower Girl doesn't tell her where she comes from or who she is. She has no other name.

But that doesn't matter. Mathilda is who she is because of Flower Girl. She is not sure if she would have been brave enough. Not on her own.

*

The girl who asks Mathilda about Flower Girl doesn't know a lot. She has asked two other people about Flower Girl. Neither of them know a lot.

So Mathilda makes tea. She cuts a few apple slices and sits down.

The girl is a good listener. She remembers every detail Mathilda tells her. She asks questions. Even after five hours of stories, she is still listening closely.

Some parts of Mathilda's life hurt. It isn't fun to remember everything. But she does tell her.

At the end, the girl thanks her. She leaves with a big smile on her lips and a mission in her heart.

# Chapter Five

# Nex

DANCING IS HIS LIFE.

In every free moment he has, he dances. On the way to school. In the breaks between classes. After school. At night, in his dreams.

The music is with him wherever he goes. It is always there, in his ear. It doesn't matter if he has headphones or not. The music is in his head.

He started dancing when he was very young. He must have been about four. Dad put on the music in the kitchen. Nex couldn't stop moving.

He's sure that what he did back then wasn't good. Not even close. But he had fun.

Dad and Papa looked at dancing schools near them. Soon, they found one. From then on, Nex had lessons once a week.

It was fun. It was amazing. But it wasn't enough.

So he used his pocket money. He bought an mp3 player first. The next month, he bought headphones.

He was six, then.

Now, he is fourteen. Dancing is his escape. No matter what is going on around him, dancing helps.

Of course, it hasn't always been easy.

In school, people laughed at him. The music was always in his ears. The beat was always in his feet. That made him different. Strange. A weirdo.

But nothing was worse than the thought of giving up dancing.

When he didn't have people, he had his music. So he danced, and danced, and danced. He never stopped.

\*

It was after a really bad day that the first flower appeared. A red poppy, wrapped around his headphones. There was a piece of paper sticking out under it.

*Follow your dreams. I am proud of you.*

*Flower Girl*

When he held the poppy close to his ear, his favorite song played.

The music surrounded him. It swept him away to another land. A land where music runs free. Where everyone dances.

Now, he has five flowers. Each plays its own, special song. Each pulls him to this land far, far away. Each makes him smile.

\*

The girl comes when he is dancing in the garden. She doesn't laugh. She doesn't point her finger. She looks like she is thinking hard about something. She is lost in her mind.

Nex knows that feeling.

He invites her in. She tells him her story. He tells her his. Even then, she never laughs.

She smiles at him. She is friendly. She asks questions. But she is never mean.

Nex opens up more. He shows her the cards that Flower Girl sent him. He dances.

They laugh together.

Then she moves on. But she promises to come back.

# Chapter Six

# Flower Girl

I HAVE COME TO understand something.

Flower Girl gives us hope. She gives us strength. Happiness. Kindness. Company. Confidence.

I do not know yet who she is. I know what she does. I know she touches people's lives. And everyone she touches becomes a better person.

But who has touched her?

Mathilda writes letters. It is sad that she is the only one.

All of us have heard of Flower Girl. Many of us have received presents from her. We like her. We think of her with smiles on our faces. But do we really care about her?

We forget her as easily as many people forget their goals.

She makes us who we are. She makes us special. She makes us different.

She makes us individuals. People who can think for themselves. People who can decide what is right and what is wrong.

She is bravery. She is kindness. She is caring. She is everything positive we humans have ever had.

But we forget her.

\*

Another flower sits on my pillow the next morning. It shimmers in silver and gold. I have never seen anything like it.

Next to it is another note. This one is folded up into a heart.

*I am not forgotten. For I am everything that is good. As long as there is any goodness left in humans, I will survive.*

# About the Author

Frida Pankiewitz is a contributing author to the Storyshares library.

# About the Publisher

Story Shares is a nonprofit focused on supporting the millions of teens and adults who struggle with reading by creating a new shelf in the library specifically for them. The ever-growing collection features content that is compelling and culturally relevant for teens and adults, yet still readable at a range of lower reading levels.

Story Shares generates content by engaging deeply with writers, bringing together a community to create this new kind of book. With more intriguing and approachable stories to choose from, the teens and adults who have fallen behind are improving their skills and beginning to discover the joy of reading. For more information, visit storyshares.org.

Easy to Read. Hard to Put Down.